Published in the United States by Clarkson N. Potter, Inc.,
225 Park Avenue South, New York, New York 10003 and represented in
Canada by the Canadian MANDA Group

Published in Great Britain by Aurum Press Limited,
33 Museum Street, London WC1A 1LD, England

CLARKSON N. POTTER, POTTER, and colophon are trademarks of
Clarkson N. Potter, Inc.

Manufactured in Belgium


Library of Congress Cataloging-in-Publication Data
Holabird, Katharine.
Angelina on stage.

Summary: Although Cousin Henry makes a pest of himself and gets all the attention
when they are asked to take roles in an adult theater production, Angelina demonstrates
her fondness for him when a crisis occurs on stage.
[1. Theater—Fiction.   2. Cousins—Fiction.   3. Mice—Fiction]
I. Craig, Helen, ill. II. Title.    PZ7.H689As 1986    [E]    86-9456

ISBN 0-517-563073-9

10 9 8 7 6 5 4 3 2 1

First Edition

# Angelina on Stage

Illustrations by Helen Craig   Story by Katharine Holabird

*Clarkson N. Potter, Inc./Publishers* NEW YORK
DISTRIBUTED BY CROWN PUBLISHERS, INC.

Angelina's cousin Henry liked to go to her ballet lessons at Miss Lilly's and join in the dancing. Henry always followed close behind Angelina copying her graceful steps, but he wiggled and wobbled and didn't look like a ballet dancer at all.

After each class, Angelina showed Henry the *right* way to
do the pliés and arabesques and twirls.

But Henry kept on dancing in his own funny way.

Then one day Miss Lilly received a letter from Mr. Popoff, the great musical director. "Angelina," said her ballet teacher, "How would you like to be a magic fairy in a real grown-ups' ballet?" Angelina was thrilled. "Oh yes!" she cried.

"It is called *The Gypsy Queen*," said Miss Lilly excitedly.
Then she turned to Henry. "Mr. Popoff needs a little elf
too, and you are the perfect size." "Hooray," shouted
Henry, but Angelina just crossed her fingers for good
luck, hoping he wouldn't do anything too silly.

At rehearsals Angelina learned to fly through the air with a special wire attached to her costume so that she looked like a fairy floating down out of the sky. Henry was supposed to scamper through the woods below looking for the fairy, but he often got mixed up and went the wrong way.

All the actors and actresses adored Henry anyway, and during the breaks the lovely Madame Zizi gave him little treats in her dressing room. Then Mr. Popoff decided that Henry should say something on stage, and Angelina felt very jealous.

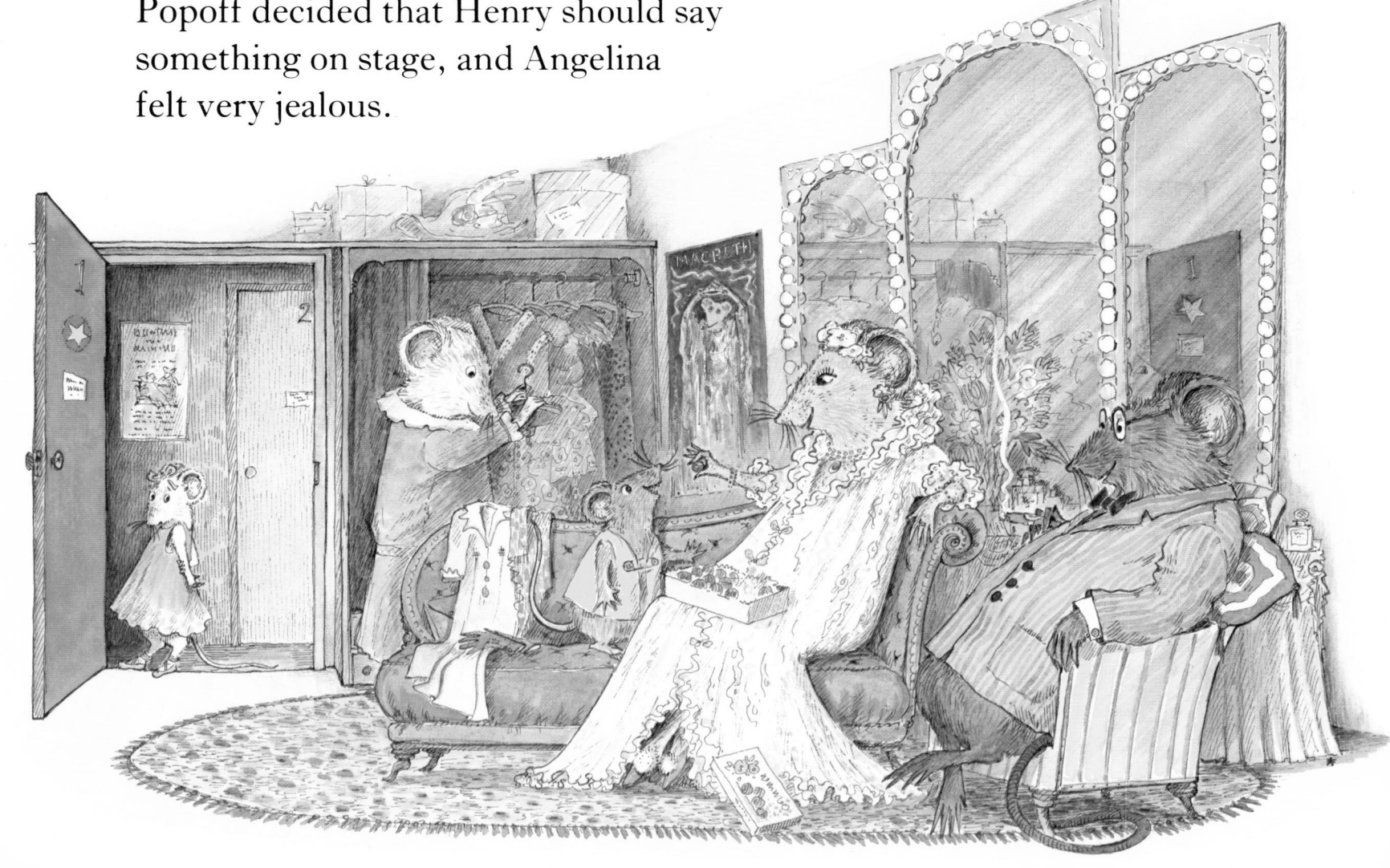

Everyone cheered when Henry came on stage and said in his little squeaky voice, "There goes my friend, the magic fairy!" But he was not so good at finding his way from the dressing room to the stage and was always getting lost.

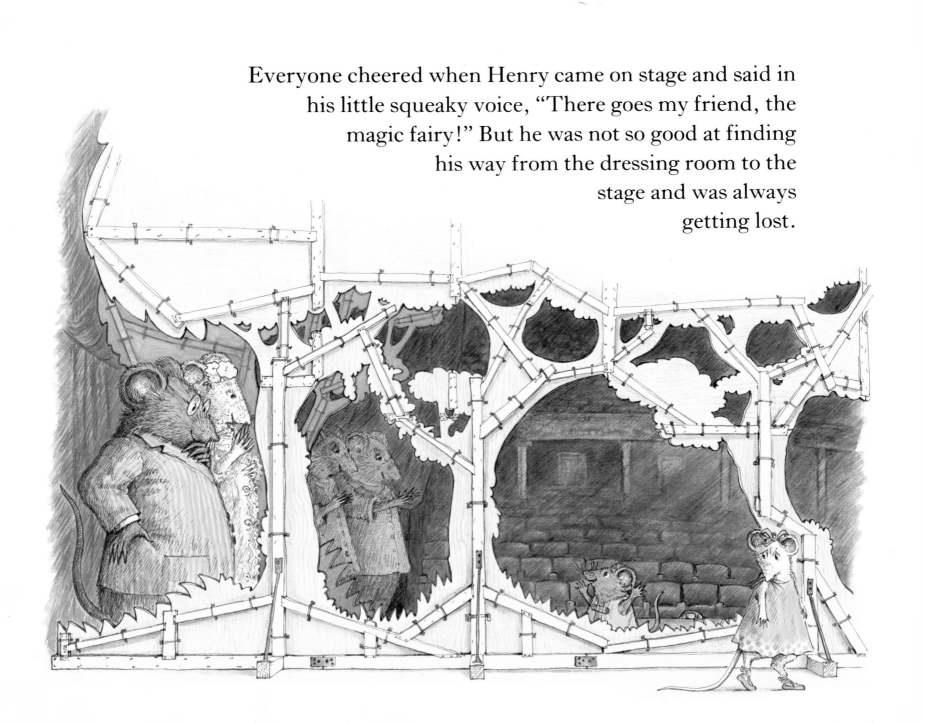

On the first night of the performance everyone back stage was very excited. Angelina waited in the wings with her crown on and her wand ready as the audience crowded into the theatre and the orchestra began to play. Madame Zizi glanced around nervously and said, "Oh dear, where's my little elf?"

Angelina ran wildly through the
corridors looking for Henry . . .

. . .and bumped into him as he was
running the wrong way down the hall.
"I got lost again!" Henry sobbed as
Angelina grabbed his hand and raced
back to the stage.

Angelina had her special wire fastened just in time.
She soared up over the trees waving her magic
wand as Henry jumped out from the wings
and skipped through the woods to the
front of the stage.

Henry turned and saw the theatre filled with lights and a sea of strange faces. He couldn't open his mouth. He just stared out at the audience.

For an awful moment nothing happened.

"Serves him right," thought Angelina, still feeling annoyed, but when she looked down and saw how terrified Henry looked she felt sorry for him.

Angelina waved her magic wand and called to Henry in a loud, clear voice, "Hello, little elf, can you see me?"

Henry looked up with relief and said, "There goes my *best* friend, the magic fairy."

At the end of the show, Angelina and Henry took a curtain call with all the actors and dancers.

The audience cheered and clapped, and the director
thanked everyone for a wonderful performance.

Madame Zizi gave Angelina some of her own roses, and Mr. Popoff smiled at her and said, "You're a fine actress and you'll have a speaking part too from now on."

Angelina was so pleased that she took Henry by the hands and waltzed around the stage with him until they were both very dizzy.